CONTENTS

Welcome to the 1997 Disney Annual!

Pedigree®
BOOKS

Published by Pedigree Books Limited,
The Old Rectory, Matford Lane, Exeter, EX2 4PS
Under licence from Disney
I.S.B.N 1.874507.63.5
Printed in the UK
© 1996 Disney

Beauty and the Beast Characters

LUMIERE
Easy-going French butler to the Beast. His humourous outlook on life makes the castle a much happier place, especially when Beast is being grumpy.

MRS. POTTS
The castle's good-natured cook and maid. She thinks the world of her son, Chip, and the two spend happy hours together in the kitchen.

CHIP
The bright little teacup who loves to help his mummy, especially when she's baking cakes! He is also very fond of Belle and looks forward to his trips out with her.

COGSWORTH
Beast's faithful English footman, in charge of the other servants. More serious than Lumière, the two often don't see eye to eye over the running of the castle.

BEAST
To teach him a lesson, a witch put a spell on this mean prince and the servants in his castle. His personality changed for the better when he fell in love with Belle.

BELLE
The book-reading village girl who came to live at the castle so that her father could go free. After a short spell of unhappiness, Belle came to love everyone in the castle, including Beast.

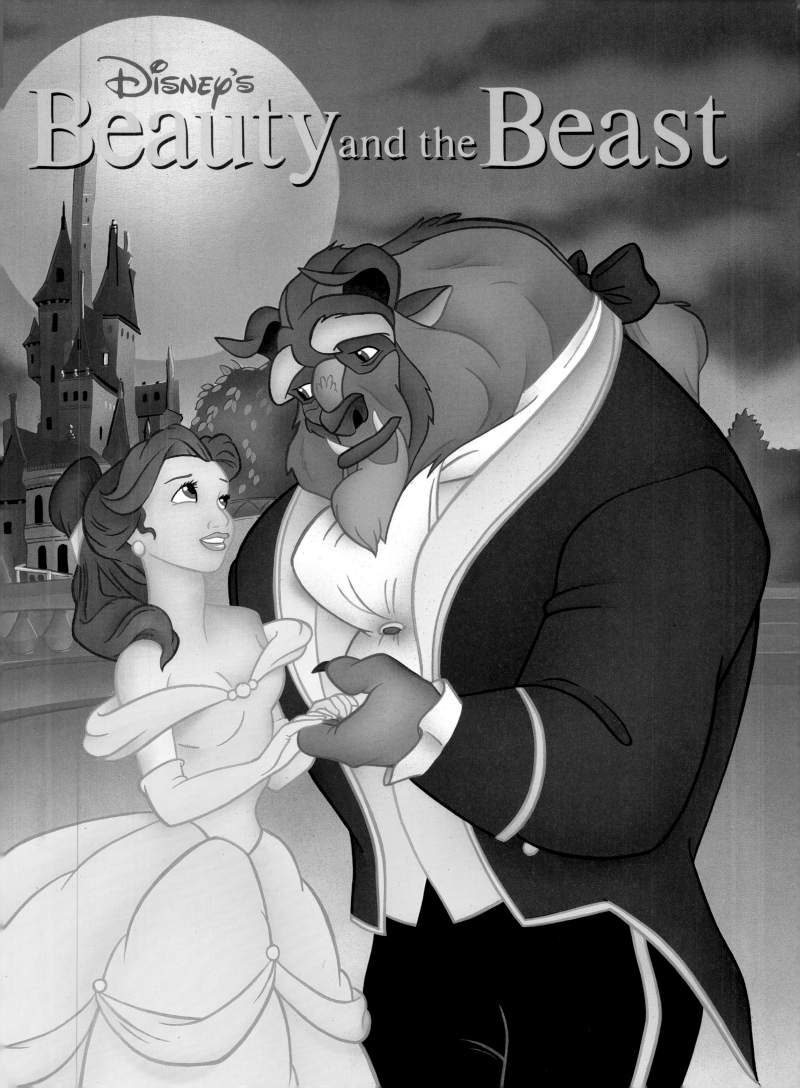

It was Christmastime. Warm light replaced the usual gloominess of the Beast's castle as Christmas candles glowed in all the windows. Belle was about to put up the rest of the decorations. She loved Christmas! As she gathered together garlands and holly, she smiled to herself as she remembered all the happy Christmas days she'd spent with her father: she would cook a delicious meal and he would make her laugh with the new inventions he'd given her as presents. Suddenly, she remembered where she was and

looked up sadly. She missed her father. She sighed and picked up the decorations, then smiled again. It was Christmas! She was going to make the best of it!

Belle decided it would be far merrier if everyone helped to put up the decorations, so she let Chip give her a hand and asked Lumiere and Cogsworth to fetch more holly. She had no idea that Beast was watching her sullenly from a distance. He let out a long, low growl.

IT'S NOT THAT I DON'T LIKE CHRISTMAS – I REALLY DO! IT'S JUST THAT...

... GROWL·L·L! I WAS AFRAID THIS WOULD HAPPEN!

WE'VE BEEN DECORATING FOR HOURS! I'M BEGINNING TO WIND DOWN!

LOOK! EVEN THE GARGOYLES LOOK FESTIVE!

GOOD! THEY'RE PROBABLY HAPPIER THAN I AM!

COGSWORTH! HOW CAN YOU GRUMBLE AT SUCH A HAPPY TIME?

Beast turned away. The others were having such fun getting ready for Christmas. He felt strange, seeing them all so happy, and wished he could join in, but something stopped him. He hung his head and was pensive for a moment, then suddenly he was overcome with rage. As the others shared a joke in the hallway, Beast thundered away unnoticed down the corridor.

The decorations were almost finished. Cogsworth was exhausted! He was sick of the sight of holly and was ready for a good rest. It seemed that they'd been helping Belle all day. She was determined that every corner of the castle would look festive and even put holly on the gargoyles! Grumpy Cogsworth though this a little excessive, but Lumière was delighted. It was going to be such a special Christmas with Belle around, he was so looking forward to it. He couldn't understand how Cogsworth could even think about complaining, but then Cogsworth always complained, even when he was happy!

EVEN THE MASTER IS CHEERF—···

GRROWL·L·L

OH MY! THE MASTER SOUNDS UPSET!

GROWL·LL

MASTER, IS SOMETHING WRONG?

WRONG? WHY, NO! CONTINUE WITH YOUR DECORATING!

I'LL HAVE TO CONTROL MY TEMPER! I SHOULDN'T HAVE GOT SO UPSET!

BUT IT'S ALMOST CHRISTMAS, AND I HAVE NO PRESENT FOR BELLE!

Lumière didn't want to miss out on the opportunity of taunting Cogsworth, so he told him to cheer up. After all, everyone was happy at Christmas, even the master! Or was he? Judging from the huge roar that came from upstairs, it seemed not. Beast often used to bellow angrily before Belle came to live at the castle, but it was quite unusual these days. Were they hearing things? No, there it was again, another long howl. The servants were worried. They hurried upstairs and burst into Beast's room to see what was wrong. Beast swung round, surprised to see them. Had he really been growling so loudly? He hadn't realised. He even looked a little sheepish as he told Lumière and Cogsworth to leave him and carry on with their preparations. Baffled, the two hesitated, then obeyed their master.

Alone again, Beast wandered over to the window and gazed out. He sighed deeply and frowned. He was cross with himself because it would soon be Christmas Day and he had no gift for Belle!

MY GIFT-WRAPPING IS ALMOST DONE!

LOOK! A LOVELY TEA COSY FOR MRS. POTTS...

... AND A SHINY NEW KEY FOR COGSWORTH!

WHAT ABOUT THE MASTER?

DO YOU HAVE A GIFT FOR HIM?

NOT YET, CHIP! I STILL HAVEN'T THOUGHT OF THE PERFECT GIFT!

Meanwhile, Belle had done all her decorating and was busy wrapping presents with Chip and Lumière. She had thought very carefully about what to give her friends at the castle. It had been cold in the castle kitchen over the past few weeks, so she had decided that Mrs. Potts would appreciate a warm tea cozy. Chip agreed that his mummy would be delighted and wished that he'd thought of it! Cogsworth had been having trouble winding up properly and was getting tired quickly, so Belle was to give him a shiny new key. She showed it to the others before wrapping it up. It shone so brightly that they might have used it as a decoration! Perhaps Cogsworth would complain a little less when he saw it!

Lumière and Chip asked Belle what she had got for their master. She still hadn't thought of what to give Beast. He'd been so kind to her recently that she wanted to give him something special. She'd have to think of something soon!

ISN'T THE TREE BEAUTIFUL, LUMIERE?

BELLE HAS BROUGHT SUCH JOY TO THIS CASTLE!

INDEED IT IS, BELLE!

I MUST GIVE HER SOMETHING SPECIAL FOR CHRISTMAS... BUT WHAT?

WAIT! I HAVE AN IDEA!

THE BEAST JOINS IN THE CHRISTMAS PREPARATIONS...

I'M GOING TO MAKE SOMETHING SPECIAL FOR BELLE!

MASTER, ARE YOU SURE YOU CAN DO THIS?

First, though, the Christmas tree needed some finishing touches. Belle and Lumière added some more shiny baubles, then lit the candles and stood back in admiration. The tree looked magnificent and it filled the room with a festive glow. It smelled wonderful, too! Belle and Lumière grinned. They'd never seen such a pretty tree!

Beast stood silently in the shadows, his eyes reflecting the candlelight. He looked at Belle and thought about how his life had changed since she came to his castle. He sighed as he tried to think of a way to repay her for her kindness. What gift could possibly be special enough to give to her? Suddenly, Beast was struck by an idea. Of course! He could *make* a present for Belle! He went to find Lumière and Cogsworth to tell them of his plan. Bewildered by this sudden show of enthusiasm, Lumière wondered whether his master had really thought this through properly. He knew that life would be difficult for all of them if the idea didn't work.

Cogsworth frowned at Lumière and scolded him for doubting their master. Of course he knew what he was doing! Beast snapped at them both to be quiet. Lumière shrugged his shoulders the way he often did. He knew Beast would end up losing his temper, but he'd done his duty, so now he would stand back and watch.

Beast set to work. He had to hurry, he didn't have much time! He set out all his tools on his workbench, then laid a piece of wood before

him. He took a deep breath, picked up a chisel, and began to carve. He spent hours carefully paring and working the wood, while Cogsworth and Lumière watched in awe. Beast had almost finished. Excited that his perfect gift would soon be complete, his concentration lapsed. As he spoke to his servants, he put a little more pressure on the chisel and...CRACK! The wood snapped. Lumière had shouted a warning, but it was too late: the damage was done.Belle's present was ruined.

Cogsworth gasped in horror. He whispered to Lumière - they knew what was coming. There was a tense silence as the servants waited for their master's rage to erupt. Beast stared at the broken piece of wood for a moment, then bellowed as he angrily raised his huge fist and brought it crashing down on to the bench. The remains of Belle's present smashed into a shower of tiny pieces that bounced across the floor. How naive of him to think that he was able to make anything so intricate!

Meanwhile, Belle and Chip were walking in the woods. It had been snowing, so the trees looked beautiful. Chip noticed how the snow sparkled and he chuckled. It reminded him of the sugar icing on his mummy's cakes! Belle noticed Chip's excitement and decided they should have some fun building a snowman. She didn't realise that Beast was still watching her from the castle window. He would never be able to join in the festivities now, not without a gift for Belle. How he hated being a beast!

Belle was making an impressive snowman. She rolled and patted and sculpted the snow until it was perfect. She and Chip stood back and admired her work. Now all the snowman needed was a face and some buttons! Chip offered to go and look for some pebbles and bounced off into the trees, singing a little nursery rhyme to himself as he went. He hadn't been gone long, when it started to snow again. Belle stopped smoothing the snowman's head and looked up. The snow was heavier than it had been earlier and was falling in huge flakes. She called to Chip, but there was no answer. The woods were silent. She looked around, but could see only trees and snowflakes.

Belle started to worry. She pulled her cape tighter around her shoulders and tramped across the snow. She peered through the trees, calling Chip's name. Still he didn't reply. What if he'd wandered off and got lost? It was dusk and the snow was falling more and more quickly.

Suddenly, Chip's chirpy little voice drifted through the trees. He was calling Belle to come and see something that he had found. Relieved that he was all right, Belle hurried towards him. She would take a quick look at whatever it was he had found, then they really should head back to the castle, before *they* turned into snowmen!

Little Chip pointed with his nose at his discovery. Belle squinted through the snowflakes. There in the snow lay a bright,

golden object. It was so shiny that it glowed against the whiteness of the snow-covered ground. Belle gasped and went to take a closer look. Chip grinned when he saw how interested she was and jumped on ahead. They both marvelled at the beautiful gem for a moment, then Belle picked it up. It felt icy and smooth in her hand and glimmered as she rolled it between her fingers. Where could such a pretty stone have come from? She polished it on her cape so that it was even more brilliant than before.

THANK YOU, CHIP! YOU'VE JUST GIVEN ME A WONDERFUL IDEA!

FINALLY I KNOW WHAT TO GIVE BEAST FOR CHRISTMAS!

BELLE HAS FOUND THE PERFECT GIFT FOR THE BEAST...

WHAT ARE YOU DOING WITH THE STONE, BELLE?

I'M CLEANING AND POLISHING IT, CHIP!

OOOOH, I GET IT! YOU'RE GOING TO MAKE SOMETHING OUT OF IT!

As Belle gazed at the stone, she suddenly smiled at Chip. Chip smiled back, even though he didn't know why they were smiling! Belle told him that she had an idea. She took one last look at the gem, then popped it into the pocket of her cape. As she picked Chip up to take him home, she thanked him. Chip snuggled down further into Belle's cape and giggled. He liked doing things to please her! Belle couldn't wait to get back and did her best to hurry through the deep snow.

Once they had returned back to the castle and warmed themselves, Belle sat at the kitchen table with the stone. She held it up to the light. She would soon have Beast's gift! Chip jumped up on to the table and watched as Belle took a soft cloth and dipped it into a jar. Then she began to rub the stone with it. Chip was a little puzzled and cocked his head to one side to get a better view. He watched for a few moments longer, then asked Belle what she was doing. So that was it! She was *making* something!

IT'S ALMOST CHRISTMAS INSIDE THE CASTLE, FINAL HOLIDAY PREPARATIONS ARE BEING MADE...

OH MY! THESE CHRISTMAS TREATS LOOK DELICIOUS, MRS. POTTS.

A FINE CHRISTMAS THIS IS GOING TO BE! I HAVE NOTHING TO GIVE BELLE!

I'VE BREWED A SPECIAL CINNAMON TEA FOR THE MASTER!

WONDERFUL! EVERYONE SEEMS TO BE IN THE HOLIDAY SPIRIT!

The following day was Christmas Eve and everyone was busy with the last of the Christmas preparations. Cogsworth had made sure that there were plenty of logs to keep the living room fire ablaze, and Lumière had checked that they had all the ingredients for Christmas dinner in the food stores. Mrs Potts spent the whole day cooking delicious festive cakes and pies, so that her baking filled the whole castle with a wonderful warm, spicy aroma. Belle was delighted when she saw the spread of tasty treats on the table and picked up a plate of mince pies to try one. She thought that she might take one up to Beast with a cup of Mrs Potts' special cinnamon tea.

Beast, however, was in no mood for tea and mince pies. It was the night before Christmas and he still didn't have anything to give to Belle. Stomping up and down the balcony, he muttered crossly to himself and made a determined effort to think clearly. He pressed his forehead against one of the cool pillars. He must think of something soon!

Beast growled so loudly in frustration that the noise could even be heard down in the kitchen. Belle looked up in dismay. What was the matter with him? He'd seemed so calm until recently. She decided to leave Beast alone for the moment. Perhaps he would cheer up later, when it was time to exchange gifts.

Upstairs on the balcony, gifts were all Beast could think about. If only he weren't a big, clumsy animal! With another huge roar, he ripped his cape from his shoulders in fury. As he hurled the cape to the ground, he saw something move in the corner of his eye. It was his brooch! Beast had torn the cape off with such force that the clasp had flown through the air and bounced off the balcony. Beast stared after it in disbelief, then stepped over his cape to look sadly over the wall. The snow was so deep, he would probably never see his brooch again! He let out a long sigh as he gazed into the darkness and listened to the others calling him from downstairs.

The servants were inviting Beast to come down and join them for the Christmas Eve celebrations. They had worked hard to make everything perfect in the castle for the festive season, and now it was time to relax and enjoy it. They had noticed Beast's recent grumpiness, but before that, he had said he was looking forward to Christmas. They called up to Beast again, thinking he hadn't heard them. Belle wondered where he'd got to, but Lumière assured her that Beast wouldn't miss their little party for anything.

Beast was growling sulkily. Not only was he without a gift for Belle, now he didn't have his brooch either! This silly Christmas business was so tiresome, he wished it were over and done with. A shiver went through him. He would have to go back inside. Lumière and Cogsworth would soon come looking for him, anyway. He picked up his cape and clumsily tied it around his shoulders, hoping no one would notice that he had no brooch. He trudged across the room and unwillingly went downstairs.

IT'S CHRISTMAS EVE AT THE BEAST'S CASTLE. BELLE AND THE ENCHANTED OBJECTS ARE EXCHANGING GIFTS...

AND THIS IS FOR YOU, LUMIERE!

NEW SCENTED CANDLES! THANK YOU, BELLE!

WHY, BEAST! LOOK AT YOU!

WHAT'S THE MATTER WITH THE WAY I LOOK?

I JUST NOTICED...

Belle and the servants had got tired of waiting for their master, so they had decided to give each other their presents without him. They gathered round the fireside whilst Belle excitedly pulled the colourful parcels out from under the tree, reading the labels before she handed them out. Mrs. Potts thought her soft tea cozy was delightful and Cogsworth adored his golden key! Lumière had just opened his box of new candles, when Beast shuffled into the room. Belle turned to smile at him, but her expression quickly changed to a puzzled frown. Beast looked miserable and his cape was tied haphazardly around his shoulders. Belle commented on his appearance, but he pretended grumpily that nothing was wrong.

Beast was annoyed that Belle had noticed his brooch was missing. Why did she have to be so observant? Now he would have to think quickly of an explanation. He couldn't possibly tell her that he'd lost it in a fit of temper!

Belle asked Beast what had happened to his brooch. Beast still couldn't think of a plausible explanation, so he simply said that he had lost it. To his surprise, Belle smiled. She believed him! Furthermore, she was holding out a neatly wrapped gift for him. Beast took the box and opened it as carefully as his monstrous hands allowed. He gasped when he saw what was inside. There lay the most beautiful brooch he had ever seen! It was far nicer than the one that had just flown out of the window and besides, it was a present

from Belle; that made it even more special. He would never lose this brooch, he would wear it always.

Beast looked up at Belle and smiled warmly as he thanked her. It was just what he wanted! Belle couldn't believe her good timing. Beast must have only just lost his brooch; he'd had it on the day before, so her gift had been perfect! She was so glad that Beast liked his Christmas present and that he'd cheered up a little.

Belle took the brooch out of its box. Realising that Beast would have trouble putting it on, she offered to do it for him. He stood still and gazed down at Belle's slender hands as she pulled the ends of his cape together and pinned the clasp on. Taking a step back to admire the gift, Belle was about to say how handsome Beast looked, but he suddenly turned away. He'd remembered that he would not be able to return Belle's kindness and felt ashamed. She'd hardly had time to ask him what was wrong, before he thrust an envelope into her hand and took to his heels down the corridor.

Belle stared after Beast in astonishment, then called out to him. He ignored her and disappeared into another wing of the castle. She stood for a moment, taken aback. What on earth was going on? He'd seemed so happy a moment ago! Then she remembered the envelope, still in her hand. She opened it quickly and began to read the neatly written note inside.

Belle frowned slightly as she read the note, then her eyes widened and she gasped as she got to the end. It all made sense now! Poor Beast! He had no Christmas gift for her and he felt disgraced. She looked up and sighed. Beast had no need to feel that way. She had been so busy thinking of gift ideas for everyone else, she hadn't even given a thought to what she might receive for herself. She wouldn't have even noticed that Beast didn't have a present for her if he hadn't made all this fuss.

Folding the note up and putting it in her pocket, Belle set off in pursuit of Beast. Down dark corridors and through creaky doors she went, searching for the master, but there was only silence. She had to find him to tell him it was all right; maybe then they could all get on with Christmas! It would be a shame for all the hard work to be for nothing. She tried calling Beast's name, but there was no reply. Belle was puzzled. He must have come this way, there was no way out. She walked on a little further and called out again.

Belle didn't know what to do next. Beast had to be somewhere nearby! There was one place she hadn't yet looked: the balcony. Surely he wasn't out there in the snow! It was worth a check, Belle decided, but then she was going to return to the warmth of the living room, Beast or no Beast. She hesitantly poked her head out into the icy air, then through the mass of snowflakes made out Beast's huge form on the far side of the balcony. Belle felt sorry for him, he looked so despondent. She would try to bring him back inside.

Beast was very still, his head hung low as he stared miserably into the darkness. He heard Belle behind him, but didn't turn to greet her, only speaking to tell her to leave him alone. Ignoring his request, Belle came nearer and put a comforting hand on his arm. Beast was so sorry that he had nothing to give Belle, after all she had done for him. He would understand if she never forgave him. With a quick shake of her head, Belle assured Beast that he couldn't possibly give her more than he'd already given her.

Beast turned to look at Belle. He could see that she really meant what she said. In fact, when he thought about it, she was right. No Christmas present in the land could match what he'd already given her. He loved her more than anything else in the world: he'd given her his heart.

They both stood for a moment in silence, as the snow gathered on their shoulders. The distant tinkle of Christmas bells from the party downstairs made them decide to go back in and rejoin the celebrations. Beast was happy at last and, as they turned to go, was able to give Belle a heartfelt Christmas greeting for the first time. Belle smiled and returned the greeting, then put her arm in Beast's to go downstairs.

The snow was falling, the celebrations were well under way and the master was happy. It was a perfect Christmas Eve at the castle, and it would be a perfect Christmas: a very merry Christmas indeed!

A page for you to colour

Aladdin characters

ALADDIN
Street-smart peasant who proved himself to be a true 'diamond in the rough'. He eventually won the love of Princess Jasmine by simply being himself.

ABU
Aladdin's companion and erstwhile partner in crime when the two lived a hand-to-mouth existence. Smart and agile, nothing gets past this monkey!

GENIE
Hilarious, fast-talking spirit, freed from eternal confinement in his magic lamp by Aladdin. The biggest, bluest Genie you'll ever see - Aladdin ain't never had a friend like him!

JAFAR
The evil adviser to the Sultan who uses his powers as a sorcerer to get what he wants. Sulky parrot, Iago, does his best to assist his master in his wicked plots.

PRINCESS JASMINE
Independent-minded daughter of the Sultan of Agrabah. Much as she loves her father, she is often perplexed by his eccentric ways.

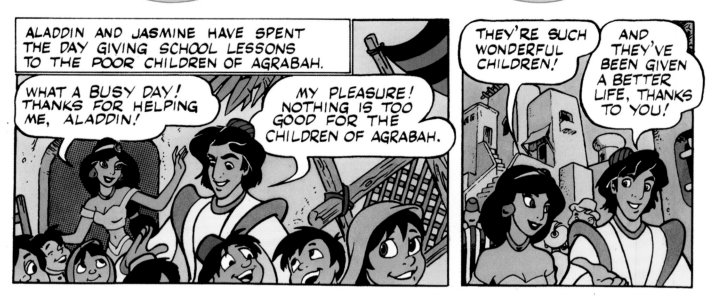

Princess Jasmine was a very caring princess. She spent a lot of her time helping other people and was especially fond of the young children of Agrabah. She had recently been spending whole days with them: reading stories to them, teaching them how to write, or answering questions on anything they cared to ask her. Sometimes she would simply entertain them and make them laugh!

Word of Jasmine's kindness soon spread, and the princess's classes got bigger and bigger. One day, so many children came along to see her that she wondered if she would cope with them all. She decided to ask Aladdin to lend a hand. He was glad to help, and told the children all about his adventures with Abu the monkey. After spending a day with the children, Aladdin could see why Jasmine adored them! Even so, the class had been noisy and excitable, so he was glad to get back to the tranquillity of the palace. Just as they had arrived back, though, Jasmine and Aladdin heard an almighty crash!

The tremendous noise had come from the Sultan's chamber. Jasmine and Aladdin broke into a run and sped through the palace. Jasmine was worried that her father had had an accident and immediately wished she had come home sooner! Aladdin reached the Sultan's room first, but Jasmine pushed past him to see what had happened. They both stood and stared in astonishment.

The Sultan's beautiful room was stuffed to the ceiling with packing crates. One of the crates had come open and spilled out toys of all shapes and sizes. There were big toys, small toys, cuddly toys, bouncy toys, clockwork toys, toys to pull along and toys to push along - there were so many toys, in fact, that the Sultan was almost buried beneath them all! Jasmine's father beamed at the worried pair, completely oblivious to their concern. He told them that the delivery had just arrived. In his eagerness to look at the new additions to his collection, he had upset one of the crates.

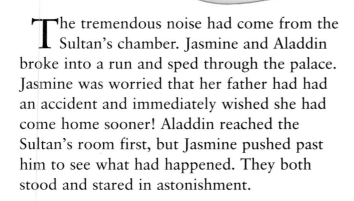

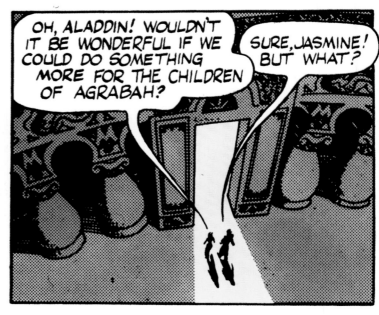

Jasmine sighed with relief as her father turned to his toys and began to play with them, whistling a merry tune to himself. The Sultan loved his toys and had a huge collection of them. Not a day went by without him taking out some of his favourite playthings. Some days he wouldn't even play with them, he would be happy enough just to look at them in admiration! Jasmine and Aladdin turned to each other and exchanged a knowing smile. They knew how the Sultan felt about his toys and understood how excited he was to receive some new ones, so they left him alone to play.

With the panic over, Jasmine's thoughts turned back to the children of Agrabah. Much as she did for them, she still felt she should do more. As she and Aladdin wandered back through the palace, they both tried to think of a way to give the children a real treat. Their discussion was interrupted by the sound of a familiar voice behind them. Who do you think it was?

It was Genie! He'd just popped up out of nowhere, as genies often do. Aladdin and Jasmine were delighted to see their old friend, but also a little surprised, as they hadn't been expecting him. Genie was just as happy to see them - and just as surprised! He hadn't meant to appear at the palace, but since he had been released from the lamp, things often didn't go the way he'd planned. He thought he was on his way to Jamaica for his holidays! Still, now he was at the palace, he thought he may as well hang around for a while.

Noticing that Jasmine and Aladdin had something on their minds, and being a nosy old genie, he asked them what the matter was. As usual, Genie got the wrong end of the stick and thought he was going to hear the pitter-patter of tiny feet! The pair managed to explain to him that they had been talking about the children of Agrabah. They told him that they wanted to do something special for them and hoped that he would think of something. If there was one person who came up with good ideas, it was Genie.

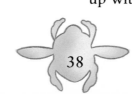

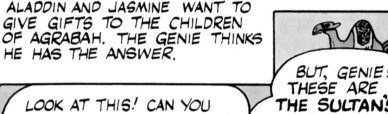

Genie felt glad that these caring people were his friends. He smiled his broad smile. Of course he knew what they could do for the children of the city! Aladdin and Jasmine looked at each other with raised eyebrows. They knew the Genie would think of something, but they hadn't expected him to do it quite so quickly! Genie told his friends to follow him and began to lead them through the palace. As they hurried along, Jasmine's mind raced as she wondered what Genie could have in store for them. Her face fell, though, as they reached their destination: her father's toy collection.

Jasmine knew Genie meant well, but his idea had turned out to be a bad one. Her father's toys meant the world to him, there was no way she could just give them away! She thought for a moment, then smiled. Their friend was a genie, he could do anything! Well, almost anything! She asked him whether he could do one of his special tricks to make some toys appear.

Genie wasn't too sure about Jasmine's suggestion. After all, he was having magic problems! He could see that the princess was relying on him, so he said he would do his best. He summoned up all the magic he could and waved his big, blue, magic hands. Hey, presto! A toy! Not! All the Genie could manage was a fish. It was a nice fish, but a fish nonetheless. You can watch a fish, but however hard you try, you can't play with it. All three were so disappointed. Genie apologised, but Jasmine was too busy worrying about the children to listen. What on earth were they going to do?

Suddenly, something dawned on Genie. It was obvious! All they had to do was ask the Sultan to part with some of his toys! His suggestion didn't go down as well as he thought it might, though. Jasmine didn't fancy the idea of asking her father to give away something so precious to him. To make things worse, who should burst in on their conversation but the Sultan himself.

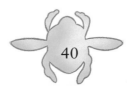

Jasmine's father had caught the tail end of the conversation and presumed that the three wanted to have a play with his toys. Aladdin told him that wasn't quite what they were thinking. There was a short pause while Jasmine thought of a way to broach the subject. The most roundabout way she could think of was to suggest to the Sultan that he might be a little fed up with his toys. Her father was flabbergasted. He picked up a clockwork elephant and stroked it affectionately. Fed up with his toys? He wound the elephant up, placed it carefully on the floor and let it go. The elephant scuttled off and crashed into Aladdin's legs so that he had to dance about to avoid it. The Sultan chuckled. He always had such fun with his toys! He would never, ever get tired of playing with them.

Jasmine sighed. She had known very well what her father would say. She turned to Aladdin. They couldn't give up yet. They had to make the Sultan change his mind, but how?

Genie fidgeted as Jasmine and Aladdin stood pondering. He was determined to help them. Maybe he should have just one more try at his magic. He shut his eyes tightly and willed a toy to appear. There was a puff of smoke and something landed in his hand. It felt solid, it felt promising....could it be...a spinning top? A boat? Oh, no! A shoe! Genie blushed with embarrassment again, but Aladdin smiled. He could see Genie was trying desperately hard to help them out. Besides, he remembered that he was lucky to be looking at Genie at all - his friend had only just escaped from being trapped in the lamp for an eternity.

Genie perked up when Aladdin reminded him of his newfound freedom and was just saying how much room he had now, when Aladdin was struck by an idea. Room! That was something the Sultan was bound to run out of soon! Their problem was solved - the Sultan would have to part with his toys if he had nowhere to put them!

Jasmine was delighted. She knew they'd think of something eventually. She and Aladdin decided to go up to her father's toy room to have look at his collection. The Sultan couldn't possibly fit many more toys in there, she felt sure of it. As they hurried along the palace corridors, she smiled to herself as she began to imagine the children's faces when she gave them the toys. They'd be thrilled!

Genie, though, was getting a little bored with all this dilly-dallying. Why didn't they just come right out and tell the Sultan about their plan? What was the old guy doing, playing with toys at his age, anyway? He tried to discuss it with Jasmine and Aladdin, but they were so busy rushing to see the toys, they didn't hear him. They had no idea either of the shock they were in for - the toy room was empty! Not even a squeaky mouse remained. They stood dumbfounded in the doorway. Where had all the toys gone? What if someone had stolen them? The poor old Sultan would be devastated!

Aladdin and Jasmine could hardly believe their eyes. As they were wondering what to do next, Genie spotted the Sultan in the palace grounds. He seemed to be running round giving orders. All three were puzzled. What was he up to? They went down to talk to him and Jasmine asked what was going on. Her father smiled and led her to a busy building site where men were hard at work fetching and carrying wheelbarrows full of bricks. Jasmine gasped as the Sultan proudly announced that this would be the new wing

for his growing toy collection! He had ordered it to be built specially. She tried to look impressed, but it was difficult to hide her dismay. Aladdin was disappointed, too. Every idea they came up with seemed to be doomed from the start.

Genie wondered if this was a good time to state the obvious. He decided it wasn't, but went ahead anyway. They could always *ask*! Lost in their thoughts, Aladdin and Jasmine continued to ignore him.

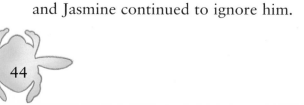

Genie was getting fed up with this. Had he suddenly become invisible or something? Why was no one listening to him? Finally, Jasmine patiently explained that asking her father wasn't an option. He was completely dedicated to collecting toys, so every single one of them was special to him. How could he bear to part with something that had taken him so long to build up? No, there was no point in even considering it. Aladdin wondered if it was worth trying to persuade the Sultan to collect something else.

That way, he wouldn't be interested in his toys anymore and he might let them go.

Later that day, yet another crate of toys was delivered to the palace. Having opened the crate, the Sultan took a box out and giggled as a funny snake popped out of it. He showed off his latest pieces to Jasmine and she obediently admired them, patting a cuddly bear on the head distractedly. Finally, she plucked up the courage to suggest that he might want to start another collection.

When Jasmine told her father that it would be a good idea to collect something rare and precious, he seemed to be rather interested. Spotting an opportunity, Aladdin suggested that it could be a special, royal collection. The Sultan's face lit up. He nodded excitedly and declared that Aladdin was right. A royal collection was a splendid idea! Jasmine and Aladdin smiled at each other triumphantly. They'd finally cracked it this time! Genie gave Aladdin a friendly pat on the shoulder and congratulated him on his brainwave, while Jasmine wandered off with her father to discuss his new collection.

They hadn't got far, though, when the Sultan announced what the royal collection was to be: toys, toys and more toys! There was nothing more rare and precious to him than his own special toys! Jasmine was astounded. How could she have got it wrong again? It seemed that the Sultan and his toys weren't destined to be parted. Now the children would never get their gifts!

Genie tried to comfort Jasmine and Aladdin. They were completely at a loss. All their plans had been in vain and they were no nearer to getting toys for the children. What more could they do? The Genie hesitated. There was still one thing they could try. He'd said it before, but he'd say it again. They could *ask*. Jasmine didn't even bother to reply this time. Aladdin sighed and tried to get it through to Genie that they couldn't ask. The Sultan was, well, the Sultan, the number one royal, the guy at the top. You

couldn't just *ask*. It wouldn't be right. It would be disrespectful.

The Genie flopped with exhaustion on to a pile of toys. This whole toy business was really beginning to get him down. He tried to waggle himself into a more comfortable position. The things weren't even any good for sitting on! He let out a long sigh. He didn't even have the energy to think anymore. He wished his magic had worked and he was sunning himself in Jamaica.

Aladdin was still trying to convince the Genie that asking the Sultan about his toys was a bad idea. Even if they did ask him, which, of course, they weren't going to, he would only give a definite no. Wearily resting his big chin in his big hands, Genie agreed. He really couldn't be bothered to do anything else! Suddenly, Aladdin had a change of heart. He decided he'd been wrong all along. The Genie jumped up in anticipation and was happy again. Al had seen sense! Finally, things were going to happen!

They ran to fetch Jasmine, who'd gone into the garden to think. Aladdin told her that he'd decided to take Genie's advice and was going to see her father that very moment to ask him to give away some of his toys. Jasmine raised her eyebrows. She saw that Aladdin meant what he said and agreed to go with him. All three friends went gingerly back into the palace. They had to do this, it was their only hope! Aladdin took a deep breath, then knocked on the Sultan's door. He closed the door gently behind him.

Jasmine and Genie waited nervously outside the Sultan's room. Genie made his ear into an earhorn shape to try and listen to what the men were saying, but it was no good. The palace doors were far too thick and the Sultan's room too large. He paced up and down outside and wondered why it was so quiet in there. Was it a good sign or a bad one? Jasmine sat down, crossing and uncrossing her legs in agitation and looking from time to time at the door. It seemed like hours since Aladdin had gone in there!

Inside, Aladdin told the Sultan all about Jasmine's lovely children and how they both wanted to give them an extra special treat. The Sultan chatted happily away for a while and even asked questions about the children in Jasmine's class. Encouraged by this warm reception, Aladdin finally asked the big question. Would the Sultan give away his toys? He waited eagerly for the answer. Of course he would NOT! The Sultan shouted so loudly that even Genie jumped. Jasmine gasped and stood up, wondering whether to intervene.

The Sultan was soon calm again. He couldn't possibly give up any of his toys, but he did want to do something for the children of Agrabah. He could see they meant a lot to his daughter and Aladdin. He grinned his royal grin and told Aladdin that he had an idea.

The two decided to keep the plan from Jasmine so that it would be a surprise. All they told her was that the whole city would soon be summoned to hear an announcement. Jasmine was baffled. What were they up to? She felt sure that she was about to be pleasantly surprised, though, and went on to the balcony to sit down. Aladdin took his place next to her and patted her hand reassuringly, as the citizens of Agrabah gathered outside the palace below. The smiling Sultan strode out and the crowds cheered and whistled to greet him. He waved for some moments and then waited for silence. He said he had some important news, but asked that the children be brought to the front first.

There was a hum from the crowd as the people turned to each other in bewilderment. The Sultan had done some funny things in his time, but this was one of his stranger requests! The children thought it was a great adventure and all ran forward as fast as they could. They gazed up at their kind Sultan expectantly, then gasped as he made his announcement. All the children were to become Royal Toy Inspectors! Every day, after their classes, they would visit the palace and 'inspect' the toys. The children danced with

joy and the rest of the crowd cheered the Sultan. He was the best Sultan a city could wish for!

It was decided that the children should make their first toy inspection immediately. They dived into the mountain of toys and began to bounce, wind up, cuddle, throw, build and squeeze the toys. The Sultan, of course, was 'supervising' and having the time of his life. It was much more fun sharing his toys. He wished he'd thought of it before!

The Genie's eyes shone as he watched the little children thoroughly enjoying themselves. He was a big, soft Genie at heart! Aladdin grinned and gave his friend a big hug. It was thanks to him that they were watching the children having fun with the toys. Genie disagreed. They'd all done it together! He was glad things had at last turned out as planned, but it was time for him to go.

Genie was going to try his magic again to take himself somewhere hot and beautiful, but first he had a present for Aladdin and Jasmine. He whipped a parcel from behind his back and handed it over. Aladdin ripped it open and laughed. It looked just like the lamp that used to be Genie's home! Genie assured them that it was just a pretty teapot, something to remind his friends of him while he was gone. Aladdin and Jasmine smiled at Genie. They didn't need a reminder, he was always in their thoughts! Genie gulped. It was time to go, before he started getting sentimental again!

They all went out on to the balcony and breathed in the cool night air. Genie said how he hated goodbyes and kissed Jasmine on the cheek, telling her to keep Al out of trouble. He then gave Aladdin one more bear hug and told him to look after his princess. He took a final deep breath, then spiralled up into the starlit sky above the palace. He stopped to look back and waved to his friends below. Aladdin put his arm round Jasmine's shoulders and they both waved a last goodbye. Genie hovered for a moment, then suddenly,

he was off. He sped past the bright full moon and disappeared through the stars into the darkness.

Aladdin and Jasmine gazed after their friend for a few seconds, wondering where he would end up this time. They would miss him, but they knew he'd be back soon. They turned to look at each other. It had been a great day after all. They'd given the children the treat they'd planned and now everyone was happy - even the Sultan!

The Aladdin Theatre

You can create your own Aladdin stories and adventures! With this easy-to-make theatre, you and your friends can take Aladdin and Jasmine on any adventure you choose.

We'll start the action off in the market place: Jasmine is anonymously exploring the streets of Agrabah. Being a princess, she has never in her life had to pay for anything. She innocently takes an apple from a fruit stall, and when she is unable to give the stallholder the money, is accused of stealing. Aladdin comes to the rescue, but a dispute has already arisen, and the two suspected thieves end up being chased by guards.

On the following pages are your cut-out characters and the backdrop to the scene described. You decide what happens next!

All you need to make your Aladdin theatre is an empty cornflake box, some scissors and some paste. Turn the page to see what to do now!

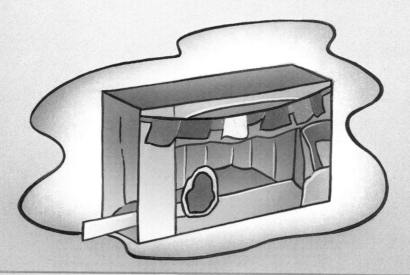

NB: You may want to do the puzzles on pages 57 and 58 before cutting these pages! Ask an adult to help with the cutting.

1 Carefully cut out both these pages, plus pages 59 and 60.

2 Cut along the dotted lines that go around the buildings and washing on these pages.

3 Carefully remove the top and bottom flaps from the cornflake box, keeping them for later. Put the box on its side.

4 The buildings and washing make the scenery at the front of your theatre, as shown on the previous page. Paste the scenery on one outer side of the cornflake box and cut away the remaining cardboard in the middle to make a stage.

5

The street and guards on pages 59 and 60 are the backdrop to your theatre. Paste these to the box's inner side so you can see it through the hole you've just made.

6

Paste this section (with the characters on it) to the cardboard you cut out when you made your stage. Cut out the characters.

7

Using the box flaps, make long strips and attach them to the characters, so that you can move them around the stage through the holes where the flaps were.

8

Get some friends, dim the lights and get ready for action! You might want to have a rehearsal first!

Free The Words!

The Genie knows how it feels to be stuck in a lamp, so he's freed these words! There are sixteen words from the story Aladdin that have just come from the lamp below. The words read up, down, backwards, forwards, diagonally - every which way! See how many of the following you can find:

**ALADDIN   JAFAR   JASMINE   IAGO
GENIE   CAVE   LAMP   WONDERS
ABU   AGRABAH   CARPET   GUARDS
SULTAN   PRINCESS   RAJAH
MARKET**

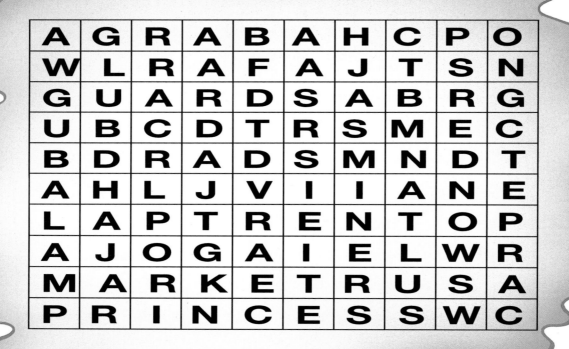

A	G	R	A	B	A	H	C	P	O
W	L	R	A	F	A	J	T	S	N
G	U	A	R	D	S	A	B	R	G
U	B	C	D	T	R	S	M	E	C
B	D	R	A	D	S	M	N	D	T
A	H	L	J	V	I	I	A	N	E
L	A	P	T	R	E	N	T	O	P
A	J	O	G	A	I	E	L	W	R
M	A	R	K	E	T	R	U	S	A
P	R	I	N	C	E	S	S	W	C

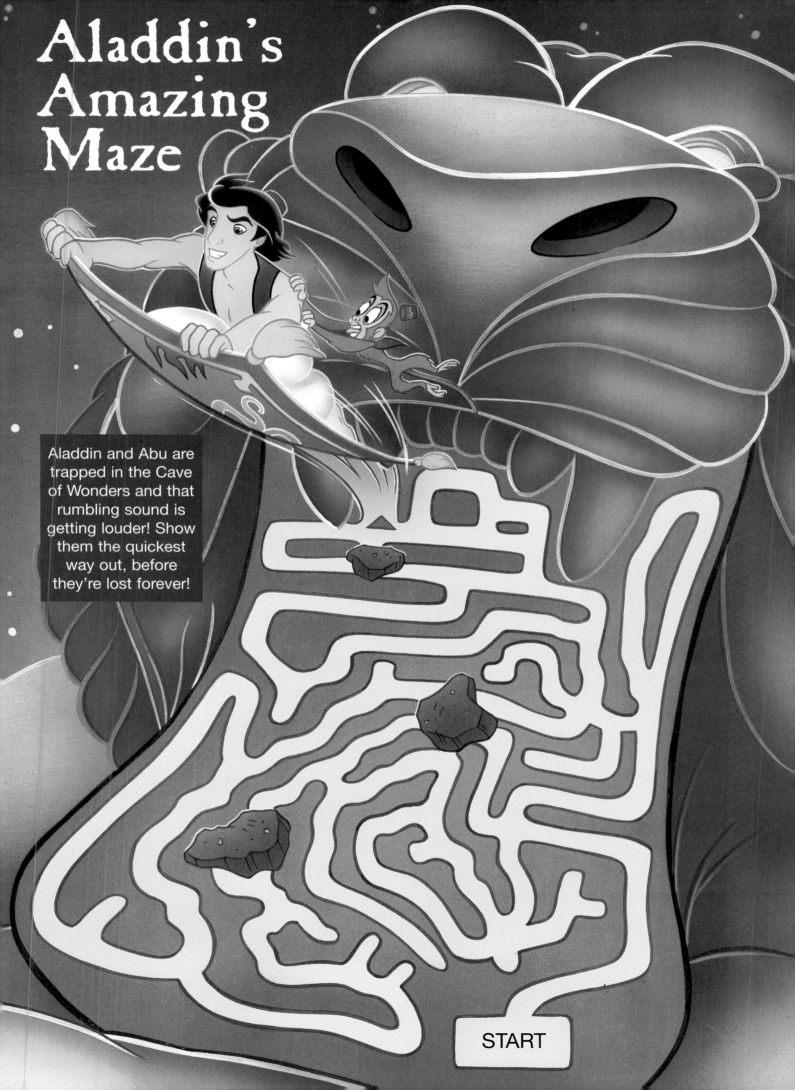

Aladdin's Amazing Maze

Aladdin and Abu are trapped in the Cave of Wonders and that rumbling sound is getting louder! Show them the quickest way out, before they're lost forever!

START

Lion King Characters

SIMBA
Heroic cub prince of the Pride Lands who just can't wait to be king. He then learns the hard way to take his place in the Circle Of Life.

NALA
Simba's fearless playmate and confidant. She can beat him in a fight, no problem! Chosen by the older lions to be Simba's future wife.

SCAR
Simba's wicked uncle. He was heir to the throne until Simba was born and has taken out his bitterness on the cub ever since.

KING MUFASA
King of the Pride Lands and Simba's father. He rules his kingdom with a firm but gentle hand and knows not to have his back turned when his brother is around.

PUMBAA AND TIMON
The wise-cracking, bug-eating duo who help Simba on the road to recovery after losing his father.

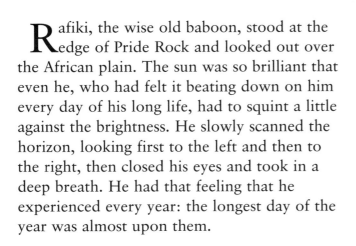

Rafiki, the wise old baboon, stood at the edge of Pride Rock and looked out over the African plain. The sun was so brilliant that even he, who had felt it beating down on him every day of his long life, had to squint a little against the brightness. He slowly scanned the horizon, looking first to the left and then to the right, then closed his eyes and took in a deep breath. He had that feeling that he experienced every year: the longest day of the year was almost upon them.

Rafiki's thoughts were interrupted by King Mufasa's voice behind him. As he turned to greet his master, he smiled as Simba the lion cub playfully scampered around the feet of his father. As Rafiki and Mufasa began to discuss the forthcoming festival, Simba asked what the solstice was. He was delighted to hear that there was going to be a special day that was longer than all the others! He was so excited that he scrambled up on to his father's back to hear more about it.

Mufasa explained that all the animals of the Pride Lands would soon be gathering to celebrate the longest day of the year. Meanwhile, Rafiki was choosing the place where the festival would be held. He stopped on a suitable patch of ground and prodded it with his staff several times before declaring it perfect. Now they needed someone to be in charge of preparing the spot for the celebrations. Mufasa said that he had already decided who that would be.

Simba raced backwards and forwards as the King wandered towards the river. He was desperate to know who his father had in mind! As they reached the river bank, Mufasa told his son to look over the edge and he would see whom he had chosen. Simba stopped short as he stared at his reflection. What did his father mean? He looked up in bewilderment. Mufasa smiled at his son and told him to get started on the preparations. Simba gasped. He was in charge!

Zazu, the King's loyal adviser, came and landed on a nearby branch to find out what was going on. Spotting him, Mufasa informed him of the forthcoming festival and ordered him to be Simba's helper. The real reason for his request was to keep an eye on Simba; he could still be a mischievous young cub at times. Besides, it would give the King a break from the bird's ceaseless chatter!

Mufasa left the pair and they set to work. They gathered up as many colourful plants, fruits and flowers as they could find, and Simba ordered the monkeys to make garlands from them to decorate the festival site with. The young cub was enjoying himself and excitedly discussed his ideas with Zazu. As they chatted, a pair of narrowed, yellow eyes watched them from a dark cranny in Pride Rock. Scar curled his lip as he cursed his nephew. Who did he think he was, supervising the preparations as if he were King? He turned away in disgust. He would have to do something about this....

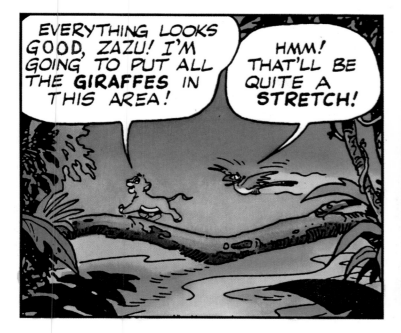

Once he'd checked the garlands and arranged their hanging, Simba set to work on organising the food. There were so many different animals coming to the gathering, they'd have to make sure they had something for everyone. Then there were some animals who didn't get on with the others, so they'd need a special space set aside; some animals, like the elephants and rhinos, needed their own space because they were the largest in the kingdom. There was so much to think about, Simba was worried he wouldn't finish it all in time!

Simba, though, was good at his new job and they were finally almost ready for the festival. He felt very proud that he'd been able to complete his father's difficult task and couldn't wait to see the King's face when he saw his work. Rafiki was most impressed when he came to see how they were getting on and complimented Simba. Scar, however, was anything but impressed, as he glared darkly from behind a bush.

Rafiki thought so highly of what Simba had done that he wanted to run and fetch Mufasa at once. Simba wasn't quite ready yet, though. He wanted everything to be perfect before his father came to look, and he and Zazu still had some finishing off to do. As they rushed around, breathlessly completing their preparations, Scar smirked from his hiding place. How silly they looked, doing all that running about for some stupid party! The truth of the matter was that Simba had made the festival site look better than it had done

for years, and Scar was jealous. He had hoped that the young cub would make a mess of things and then be out of favour with the King, but now....

Scar paced back and forth as he pondered over his problem. What a nuisance Simba was! Until he came along, Scar had been sure that he himself would become King one day. Now he had no chance. As he slunk away, Scar mumbled to himself as he thought of a way to disgrace young Simba.

Simba and Zazu had finished their preparations at last. Simba trotted around the festival site, admiring the beautiful decorations and feeling quite proud of himself, whilst Zazu flew along behind him and agreed that their work had been a great success. The King's adviser had not previously relished the thought of spending the afternoon with Simba: the young cub would usually outsmart him, then do something dreadfully naughty and they would both be in trouble with the King. Today, however, had been most enjoyable. Simba had shown himself to be an ideal future king and it looked as if the forthcoming solstice celebrations would be the best ever. Now everything was in place, it was time to give the area a final check before Mufasa saw it.

As the pair hurried off, Scar watched disdainfully from a nearby ledge, then sniggered. He had just thought of a perfectly horrible plan to give both Mufasa and Simba a nasty shock!

Scar turned on his heels and broke into a run. He didn't have much time! He hoped that the hyenas were at home, and not out doing the disgusting things that hyenas do. As he approached the hyenas' lair, he could hear Banzai's shrieking laughter, followed by hysterical cackling from Ed and Shenzi. The hyenas were most definitely in.

The hyenas' laughter stopped abruptly as they saw Scar and asked him what he wanted. The King's brother had come to them before with empty promises, so they had learnt to be wary of him. However, Scar's usual combination of charm and menace soon had them ready and willing to carry out whatever wicked plan it was he had in mind. Even so, the hyenas were still a little shocked when they heard what Scar wanted them to do. Ruin the festival site? But it looked so pretty! It must have taken someone hours to decorate it. All became clear when they were told who that someone was: Simba. Scar was always hatching plots against his nephew.

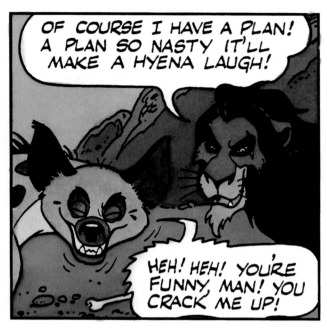

Banzai saw a problem with Scar's idea: the festival area was huge, there was no way they could destroy the whole lot before the animals arrived. They were good, but they weren't that good! Scar gave Banzai a scornful look, before announcing that he had already thought of a plan that was so wicked, even he thought it so. The hyenas guffawed in anticipation and waited to hear what Scar had been plotting. Fickle as they were, they had already forgotten how they had come unstuck with his ideas before.

Meanwhile, Simba had just finished making small changes to the party site. Zazu was beginning to get impatient and tried to persuade Simba that it was time they went to fetch Mufasa, but Simba still wanted to check everything one last time. Suddenly, Zazu was distracted by an unexpected movement to his right and stopped talking in mid-sentence, which was very unusual for him. Frowning, he turned to see what it was, but all was still again. What could it have been? The area had been deserted only a moment ago.

Zazu was suspicious, and as the King's adviser and royal childminder, it was his duty to check that nothing was amiss. He flew nearer to the place where he thought he'd seen something move and told Simba to follow him. They scanned the area, but found nothing. Zazu could have sworn that he had spotted a hyena, and hyenas were always up to no good, but it seemed that he had been seeing things. Perhaps all this festival business was going to his head. The very thought of hyenas, though, made him feel on edge.

Suddenly, the two were startled by a gopher erupting out of the ground. Scattering soil everywhere, he saluted and announced that he was bringing a message from his master, King Mufasa: Simba and Zazu were to go back to Pride Rock at once. Zazu regained his composure, then gave the messenger one of his stern rebukes for alarming them, but he was secretly relieved. At least Simba would now have to leave the festival site and go home - he very rarely disobeyed his father.

Zazu had not been imagining things. The hyenas *were* skulking around and they *were* up to no good. As Scar led them along an old tree that had fallen across the river, he stopped and looked down at the rushing water below. The unexpected stop made the chattering hyenas crash into each other and scrabble around on the log to regain their balance. Scar gave them a reproachful look and waited for them to be still, then explained why he had brought them to the river: they would be using it to flood the party area.

Since the river was a fair distance from the festival site, this was too much for the hyenas to understand. Scar was patient with them. His plan was, of course, ingenious, and he could hardly expect animals of far less intelligence to grasp it. He told his henchmen that they would be able to divert the river in any direction they wanted, provided they chose the right place. The hyenas were delighted with the plan and eagerly followed Scar as he looked along the bank for a suitable spot.

Scar surveyed a stretch of the river, then selected the part they would be working on. The hyenas couldn't wait to get started and bounded around excitedly, but then realised that they didn't know what it was they were supposed to be doing. They awaited Scar's instructions. He pointed to an enormous pile of boulders at the top of the river bank and ordered them to run up and push a few down. This would set the whole pile rolling down to the river and change the direction of its flow.

The hyenas gleefully set to work and set first several, then hundreds of rocks bouncing down the bank. They cackled hysterically as they watched the boulders plop into the river and form a new mound. It wasn't long before the river changed direction and began to cascade towards the festival area exactly as planned. Scar smiled smugly as he imagined the devastation it was going to cause. His idea had worked perfectly, but then he knew it would. He was such a clever lion and would, after all, one day be king.

GOODY! I'VE ALWAYS WANTED TO MAKE A BIG SPLASH!

ZAZU! WHAT'S THAT NOISE?

IT SOUNDS LIKE IT'S COMING FROM THE FESTIVAL SITE!

WE'VE GOT TO GET DOWN THERE!

OH, NO!

ROAR!

Scar rubbed his scrawny paws together and sniggered. Now all he had to do was sit back and watch the river do all his dirty work for him. Simba's pretty little party ground would soon be awash with river water and there was nothing the impudent cub could do about it! What on earth would Mufasa say when he saw what a mess his beloved son had made of things?

Simba and Zazu had almost reached Pride Rock when Simba's ears suddenly pricked up and he stopped, turning his head in the direction that they'd just come from. He could hear the sound of rushing water in the distance. Zazu could hear it, too, and immediately began to fear the worst. Something was definitely wrong! The two turned on their heels and sped back down towards the site. They had almost reached it when they a gush of water passed them. The sound of the river was now deafening as it bubbled and frothed its way to its destination.

Simba gasped, then began to run even faster. The river was rushing straight towards the festival site, the one that had taken him and Zazu weeks to decorate. He had to do something! He had to save all his hard work, otherwise he would have nothing to show his father and he would be considered a failure. Furthermore, the animals were due to arrive soon for the festival! Poor Simba raced desperately to try and overtake the river. He thought that if he could get ahead of it, he might stop it before it did any damage.

As the cub dashed in front of the path of the crashing river, Zazu caught him up. When he realised what Simba was trying to do, he was so astonished, he could barely speak. The silly little lion! He actually thought he could hold up the water! Zazu managed to blurt out a warning, seconds before he saw Simba engulfed by the relentless river. Swooping down to the surface, he began to frantically search for a sign that Simba was all right. He wasn't even sure that he could swim! Zazu called out Simba's name despairingly.

Just as Zazu felt panic rising within him, there was a light splash as Simba's head popped up out of the water. He grinned a soggy grin and assured Zazu that he was all right. Zazu landed on a log and breathed a happy sigh of relief, but then the pair's faces fell as they realised what had happened. The entire festival area was waterlogged and all their preparations had been destroyed. They both surveyed the scene dejectedly and wondered what they were going to do now - they only had a day to think of something.

Their conversation was interrupted by Scar, who began to scoff at Simba's attempts at party preparations. They turned to face him and Zazu eyed the King's brother suspiciously. He always seemed to turn up when something terrible happened. It could hardly be mere coincidence that he had appeared immediately after this disaster; he was probably behind the whole incident. Scar raised his eyebrows serenely and feigned offence at the accusation. As if he could be capable of such a thing!

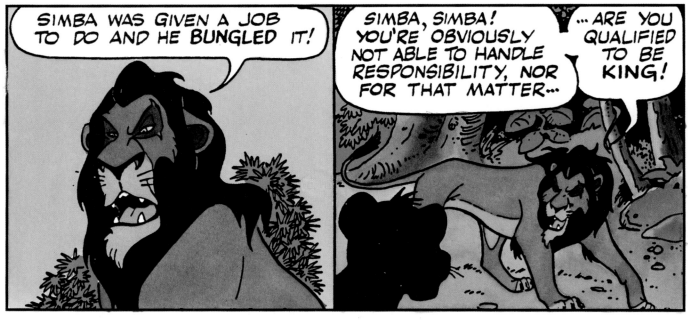

Scar suggested that young Simba had taken on more than he was capable of in trying to prepare for the Pride Lands' festival. He was only a simple little cub, after all. Zazu was now sure that Scar had caused the flood; he was always looking for ways of belittling the King's son, to put himself in a better light. Zazu became more agitated as he repeated his accusations, whilst Scar stayed calm and mocked the poor bird's rantings. He then turned to Simba and continued to gloat over his failure to do the job assigned to him. The young cub sat and looked sadly at his uncle, listening to what he had to say.

As Scar finished his tirade by telling his nephew that he was not at all fit to be king, Simba hung his head in shame. Seeing that his speech had had the desired effect, Scar smiled with satisfaction before leaving Simba and Zazu with their arrangements in ruins. Zazu flapped about in frustration, still furious with Scar, then calmed down when he saw how miserable Simba looked.

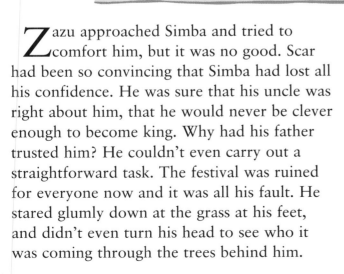

Zazu approached Simba and tried to comfort him, but it was no good. Scar had been so convincing that Simba had lost all his confidence. He was sure that his uncle was right about him, that he would never be clever enough to become king. Why had his father trusted him? He couldn't even carry out a straightforward task. The festival was ruined for everyone now and it was all his fault. He stared glumly down at the grass at his feet, and didn't even turn his head to see who it was coming through the trees behind him.

It was Rafiki, and he had been listening to what Simba was saying as he approached. Rafiki was an ancient baboon. He was old even when Scar was born, and had watched the naughty cub grow up into a wicked lion, so he was only too familiar with these nasty tricks. Smiling down at Simba, he assured him that he was more than capable of being king. Then he told him that there was no problem. There was only a problem for as long as Simba accepted that there was one. All he had to do was think.

Simba looked puzzled as he listened to Rafiki's advice. He gazed pensively into the distance; all he had to do was think... Suddenly he was bouncing about in excitement as an idea came to him almost immediately. He knew exactly what he had to do! Simba began to race back towards the festival site, telling Zazu to follow him. They had work to do and they had to do it quickly! Zazu flapped around in a panic for a moment, then followed Simba as ordered. Rafiki watched them go and nodded his head wisely.

It was time for the solstice celebrations. All the animals in the Pride Lands were looking forward to the party. Everyone, from the elephants down to the ants, thundered in one enormous herd towards Pride Rock in search of the festival site. As it neared its destination, the whole herd surged forward as everyone tried to get a look at the party area. It then came to a sudden stop as the animals all stared in disbelief. They'd never seen anything like it! Where there had been land, there was water; a vast lake of water!

The animals were delighted. It was terribly hot, so after that long, dusty journey, a refreshing swim was just what they needed! To make things even more pleasant, Simba had decorated the new water hole and made sure there were plenty of logs to play on. The elephants and giraffes waded slowly into the cool lake, whilst the cheetahs and zebras bounded in and began to swim. The monkeys screeched to each other as they gleefully swang on vines above the surface before leaping in.

Once they were all in, the animals began to have such fun: the elephants sucked up water in their trunks and sprayed it over themselves and the other animals; the monkeys splished and splashed each other; the young animals swam underwater, then squirted water jets from their mouths when they emerged. Everyone agreed that these were the best celebrations they'd ever had. This was far better than fighting for a place in the shade. Why had no one thought of it before? The party was a great success!

Simba and Nala watched the fun from a grass mound and giggled at the animals' revels. Mufasa, who was sitting beside them, congratulated Simba on coming up with such an innovative idea for the festival. He looked down proudly at his son and smiled, before turning back to watch the animals of his kingdom enjoying themselves. Scar and the hyenas sat glumly on a log, refusing to take part in the jamboree. The King's brother, furious that his plan had backfired, glowered at his nephew and let out a long growl. He

had just begun to rant bitterly about it all, when suddenly he lost his balance and fell into the lake with a loud splash. The whole party erupted in peals of laughter as a humiliated Scar emerged, spluttering, from the water that he'd gone to such trouble to provide.

Simba laughed loudest. He was glad he'd listened to wise old Rafiki and not his uncle. From then on, whenever he had a problem, he would always remember: all he had to do was think!

A page for
you to
colour

Mickey and The Runaway Brain

A STORY TO COLOUR

1

As the sky turned black, thunder crashed around Mickey Mouse's house. Only flashes of lightning lit the murky street outside.

"Pluto, look out!" cried Mickey.
From the street, strange sounds could be heard as Pluto barked excitedly, leaping over furniture like a lunatic!

Indoors, Mickey was playing a new computer game on his televison screen. Unaware of the noise he was making, he cried, "Take that - and that! And catch one of these, buster!"
Mickey didn't even hear the doorbell ring as he prodded and punched the joystick.
"Mickey?" called Minnie Mouse, letting herself into the house.
No response. Mickey was too busy getting rid of the villains in his game to notice anything!
Stepping in front of the television, Minnie blocked Mickey's view.
"You've forgotten what day it is, haven't you?" gasped Minnie.
"Oh, nooooo! Certainly not! Er, forgot what?" Mickey stammered.
"Our anniversary!" snapped Minnie.
"Oh, yeah - anniversary! Um, what anniversary would that be?" gulped Mickey.

2

"Our very first date, that's all!" sighed Minnie.
Just then, Mickey spotted a newspaper advert, showing a 'two for the price of one' golfing holiday.
"Fooled you!" he laughed. "I've got everything planned - take a look!"
Minnie wasn't impressed as Mickey went on, "You and me, out in the sun, fresh air, blue skies, for eighteen glorious..."
"...days in Hawaii? Oh, Mickey!" gushed Minnie.
Mickey almost fainted when he looked at the advert Minnie had spotted. It was for a Hawaiian cruise, costing £999.99!
"Aloha!" called Minnie, rushing off to search for holiday clothes bargains.

"What am I going to do, Pluto?" sighed Mickey. "You need plenty of moolah to hula!"
Pluto pushed the 'wanted ads' forward and pointed.
Mickey's eyes fell upon an advert which read: 'Earn £999.99 for a mindless day's work!'

3

4

5

Mickey had no time to lose. He raced over to the address given in the advert and knocked on the door. Suddenly, the pavement opened up - and Mickey fell through a trap-door!

He landed in a chair and clank! clank! clank! - steel clamps locked over Mickey's hands, legs and body.

"Doctor Frankenollie at your service!" smirked a crazy-looking scientist. "So you're here for the job, huh?"

"Er, I've changed my m-mind about the job!" gulped Mickey.

"Ahh, this is not just a job...it's an adventure!" grinned Doctor Frankenollie. "Let me introduce your co-worker - I made him myself!" As the mad doctor pressed a remote control button, the floor opened - and a raving monster appeared!

Before Mickey had time to blink, Doctor Frankenollie pushed a metal helmet on to his head and pressed a computer button. He grinned as an x-ray of Mickey's head appeared on a screen. "Daddy's found you a new brain, Julius!" he smiled.

"Wait! You're not going to...?" gasped Mickey.

"Put your brain in Julius's body? Of course I am! Ha! Ha! Ha!" cackled the mad doctor.

As Doctor Frankenollie flicked another switch, electrical currents surged through Mickey's head. A loud explosion followed - and the doctor disappeared in a puff of smoke!

"Ooh, I don't feel myself. I..." wheezed Mickey.

It didn't take Mickey long to work out that he wasn't himself! His brain was now inside the body of the monster!

With a roar, the monster sprang forward.

"Uh, you monster...me Mickey. Mickey Mouse! You know?" said Mickey, trying to soothe Julius.

"Hmmm?" muttered the monster, examining his strange new body.

"Look in my wallet and you'll see who I am!" gasped Mickey.

"There, see? That's me with my girlfriend, Minnie!"

"Oh...Minnie!" sighed the monster.

"That's right! And she likes my body and my mind - preferably in the same place!" said Mickey, trying to take back his wallet.

The monster went berserk, screaming Minnie's name over and over as he scrambled up Mickey's legs. Catapulting over the top of Mickey's head, the monster escaped through the sewer gate.

Still mumbling Minnie's name, Julius peered over the edge of a building. Down below, he spotted Minnie as she walked into a swimwear shop.

As Minnie admired a bikini, the monster burst through the door!

"Why, Mickey! I was just wondering if you'd like this little thing I've found to wear on the beach!" smiled Minnie.

The monster growled, his eyes almost popping out of his head.

"Ah, ah, ah...not until we're on the boat!" scolded Minnie with a cheeky smile.

As the monster lunged at Minnie, Mickey crashed through a window and grabbed him. Not realising that Mickey was now inside the monster's body, Minnie threw anything she could lay her hands on at him - and freed the monster.

"C'mon, Mickey - let's get out of here!" she gasped.

"That was close, but I think we've lost him!" puffed Minnie, as she and the monster ran through the streets.

Minnie was wrong! Slowing down just long enough to push a coach from his path, Mickey soon caught up.

"Put me down, you...you, MONSTER!" screeched Minnie, as Mickey plucked her off the ground.

"Hey, stop that! It's me - Mickey!" spluttered Mickey, as Minnie punched him on the nose.

"Mickey? It really is you!" gasped Minnie.

"Don't look now, but I think we have company!" cried Mickey, as the monster hurtled towards them on the bonnet of a speeding car.

"Hang on!" yelled Mickey, using a crane to swing to the top of a building.

"You'll be safe here," Mickey told Minnie, leaving her on the roof.

"Go get him, Mickey!" called Minnie, as Mickey swung away.

As the monster tried to escape, Mickey swung down and scooped him into the air.

"Raghhhh!" roared the monster.

Tugging at a bucket, the monster released a pile of bricks, which crashed straight on to Mickey's head.

"Gnnnng!" gasped Mickey, losing his balance and falling from the crane.

20 21 22 23 24 25 26 27

The pair landed on power lines, causing an electric surge. As their brains glowed, Mickey and the monster were catapulted up into the air, back towards the building.

The monster grabbed Minnie and all three soared on towards a huge billboard! Then...CRASH!

Luckily, the electrical current had put Mickey's brain back inside his own body again.

"Oooooh! Minnie?" mumbled Mickey.

"Mickey? Oh, Mickey!" sighed Minnie.

But things weren't back to normal yet! The monster was still clutching Minnie in his huge hand.

"Let her go!" shouted Mickey.

With a swift flick of his free hand, the monster sent Mickey over the side of the building.

"Oh, noooo!" cried Minnie. "Mickey's disappeared!"

"Not quite!" smiled Mickey, popping up on a window cleaner's platform.

Using a long-handled mop, Mickey pole-vaulted over the monster, landing on the billboard. Then he swiftly lassoed one end of his rope to the moving arm of a hula girl, and wrapped the other end round the monster!

"Agaaah!" cried Minnie, as the monster dropped her over the edge. Swinging to her rescue, Mickey safely landed back on the roof.

Standing beneath the broken Hawaii billboard, Mickey and Minnie hugged each other with relief.

"I guess that billboard's just like our anniversary - ruined!" sighed Minnie.

Trying to escape, the monster took a step backwards - and fell over the edge of the building! The rope, which was still attached to the hula dancer, made Julius boing up and down like a giant yo-yo!

"Happy anniversary, Minnie," blushed Mickey, as he and Minnie later dangled their feet in warm, blue waters. They were going on their dream holiday at last!

"Oh, you're so romantic!" smiled Minnie.

"I know!" grinned Mickey, as they headed towards Hawaii. They'd persuaded a friend to pull them along on a raft. Do you know who that friend was? Julius! He wasn't such a monster, after all!

Pocahontas Characters

JOHN RATCLIFFE
The selfish Governor of the Jamestown settlement who can think of nothing but finding gold. Often accompanied by his beloved pug dog, Percy.

CAPTAIN JOHN SMITH
The bold English explorer, Captain of the Susan Constant sailing ship, who fell in love with Pocahontas soon after his arrival in the New World.

CHIEF POWHATAN
Chief of the Indian village and father to Pocahontas. A brave but sensitive warrior, he is proud of his courageous daughter.

POCAHONTAS
The free-spirited Indian princess who always follows her heart. Her two friends, Meeko the raccoon and Flit the hummingbird, are usually at her side.

MEEKO
Pocahontas's playful raccoon companion. His constant search for food usually gets him into mischief!

POCAHONTAS, THE GREAT SPIRIT HAS SMILED ON US WITH AN ABUNDANT HARVEST.

YES, FATHER! OUR STOREHOUSES ARE OVERFLOWING!

BUT THE JAMESTOWN SETTLEMENT WILL NOT HAVE A VERY MERRY CHRISTMAS...

IT GIVES ME COMFORT TO KNOW NO ONE WILL GO HUNGRY THIS WINTER.

I ONLY WISH THAT WERE TRUE!

THE JAMESTOWN SETTLEMENT...

WIGGINS! I MUST SEE GOVERNOR RATCLIFFE, AT ONCE!

WELL, SMITH! DO YOU BRING ME WORD OF GOLD?

A chill December wind blew around Pocahontas and made her pull her shawl tighter around her shoulders. She and her father were gazing out over their land, its soil as solid as stone from the cold. They thought about how lucky they were to have had such a good harvest, which had given them twice as much food as they needed to last them the winter. Powhatan was grateful that the spirits had treated them so well this year; past winters had not been so easy. At least he could be sure that lack of provisions would not be a problem for his people. They already had the settlers to worry about, after all.

Pocahontas was also thinking about the settlers, but for a different reason. She knew that their food supplies were running low. They hadn't found out about how to grow food when they arrived, and there certainly hadn't been room on the ship to bring enough supplies with them. Her thoughts turned to one settler in particular: Captain John Smith.

WE'VE A MORE SERIOUS PROBLEM, SIR! OUR FOOD SUPPLIES ARE LOWER THAN I REALISED!

THE MEN SHOULD HAVE BEEN PLANTING FOOD INSTEAD OF DIGGING FOR GOLD!

YOU QUESTION MY AUTHORITY, SMITH? REMEMBER, AS GOVERNOR I AM IN CHARGE HERE!

WITH ALL DUE RESPECT, SIR, THIS SETTLEMENT WILL NOT SURVIVE THE WINTER WITHOUT FOOD!

CIVILISED MEN ALWAYS FIND A WAY, SMITH! SEE TO IT!

Whilst Pocahontas was worrying about John Smith, he was telling Governor Ratcliffe of the settlement's food problem. Disappointed that the soldier wasn't bringing him long-awaited news of a gold find, the Governor had no interest in what he had to say. John Smith struggled to control his anger at Ratcliffe's indifference. It was the settlers' obsession with finding gold that had caused the problem in the first place. He pointed out that if they had all concentrated their energy on growing food, rather than searching for

gold, they would now have reaped enough to survive the winter.

Ratcliffe bristled at this accusation of incompetence and reminded the Captain of his superior position. John Smith sighed wearily and tried one last time to make clear to the Governor the gravity of the situation, but his efforts were in vain. Ratcliffe had made up his mind that the problem had nothing to do with him, and he ordered John Smith to deal with it.

I REGRET SOME MAY GO HUNGRY THIS WINTER, PERCY! BUT WE'LL NOT BE AMONG THEM!

PERCY

WE'VE HIDDEN OUR OWN SUPPLY OF FOOD ON THE SHIP! HEH! HEH!

MEEKO, IF I'M TO HELP THE SETTLERS I'LL HAVE TO THINK OF SOMETHING FAST!

IT'S DIFFICULT TO KNOW WHAT PATH TO TAKE

The reason for Ratcliffe's apparent lack of concern was that he didn't, in fact, have to worry about food for the winter. Neither did his pampered dog, Percy. The selfish Governor had suspected that there might be a shortage once winter arrived, and had decided to make sure that he had his own private food supply, just in case. It was now hidden away in the ship, which was anchored nearby. He offered his fat pet another bone and stroked its wrinkly forehead as he sniggered and congratulated himself on his good planning.

Pocahontas swiftly paddled her canoe down the river as she tried to think of a way to help the settlers get food. Her friend, Meeko the raccoon, looked up at her brightly as she told him of their plight. She often travelled down the river if she had a problem to solve. The lapping of the water soothed her and she could listen to the wind's guidance, away from the distractions of the village. Today, however, she could not seem to think clearly. She would have to ask for advice, and there was only one place to go for that.

BUT I THINK I KNOW WHO CAN HELP ME!

HELLO, CHILD! I'VE NOT SEEN YOU IN A WHILE!

GRANDMOTHER WILLOW! I DON'T KNOW WHAT TO DO!

THE VISITORS LACK FOOD WHILE WE HAVE PLENTY!

HOW CAN I HELP WHEN THE SETTLERS AND OUR PEOPLE FEAR EACH OTHER?

LISTEN TO YOUR HEART, POCAHONTAS YOU'LL FIND THE ANSWER THERE

Whenever Pocahontas needed help, she went to a magical place in the forest, the enchanted glade. There she could tell her problems to the sage old tree spirit, Grandmother Willow. Sometimes she would go simply for a chat; Grandmother Willow always had something interesting to say. Pocahontas decided to go and explain the settlers' situation to the spirit and see what she thought. She let her canoe slide up the river bank and jumped out. Meeko scuttled after her as she approached the ancient tree.

Grandmother Willow was delighted to see Pocahontas. She hadn't been expecting to see anyone before the spring, now that there was snow on the ground. She could see that there was something troubling the girl. With a worried frown, Pocahontas told the ancient spirit that her people had an abundance of food, whilst the settlers were certain to starve during the winter. She knew that the Indians would never agree to give any of their food to the visitors, who in turn would never agree to accept it.

GRANDMOTHER WILLOW! YOU'VE GIVEN ME THE ANSWER!

THE ANSWER WAS ALWAYS THERE, POCAHONTAS! YOU ONLY HAD TO LISTEN!

Grandmother Willow listened and nodded wisely. She smiled warmly at her favourite Indian girl, impressed by her eagerness to help others. It was no wonder Pocahontas was so fond of John Smith; he had come to meet Grandmother Willow recently and she had thought him most charming. She realised that it would be a terrible thing for the settlers to go hungry when there was food to feed them, but concluded that she could not tell Pocahontas what to do; the girl had to search in her own heart for the solution.

Pocahontas was taken aback for a moment. She had been expecting to hear the answer to her problem, and had no idea that the solution was already within her. Contemplating Grandmother Willow's wizened features, she breathed in, then looked up into the dense foliage of the spirit. The wind blew through the leaves and Pocahontas tried listening again for guidance. Suddenly, it all became clear to her. She gasped and looked back at Grandmother Willow. The spirit was right, she did already have the answer!

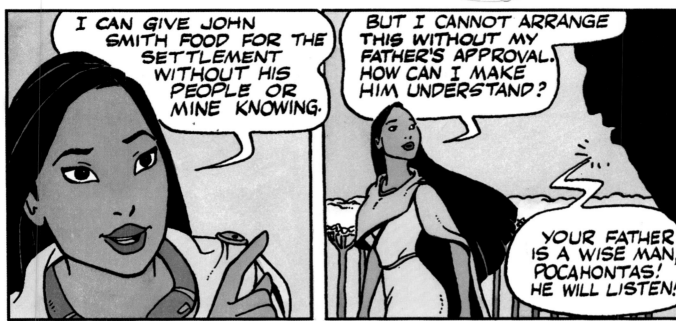

It was true that the Indians would no more give their food than the settlers would accept it, but if Pocahontas and John Smith could transfer the food secretly between them, neither people need know! That way, no food would be wasted and no one need go hungry. There was one person who would know if food went missing, though: Powhatan. Pocahontas had no choice but to tell him of her plan and persuade him to agree to it. Grandmother Willow assured her that the Chief would understand.

However, a doubtful frown crossed Powhatan's face as he listened to his daughter plead with him to help the settlers. The Chief wasn't happy that the settlers were short of food, but he had to think of his own people. The visitors did, after all, have only themselves to blame. Pocahontas wished there were no hostility between the peoples. She knew her father spoke the truth, but she could not believe he would stand by while people starved. She decided now was the time to suggest her plan.

Powhatan's doubtful frown gradually left his face as he listened to his daughter. He felt proud that she was able to look beyond the differences between her own people and the settlers; she simply saw fellow humans in need. Realising that they would be the only ones to know about the plan, he decided that he would give his permission for it to go ahead. He smiled very slightly and affectionately touched his daughter's hair. Waiting for him to speak, she looked at him hopefully. When he gave his agreement, she beamed at him and quickly gave him a grateful hug.

Pocahontas's face was suddenly serious as she heard the voice of Kocoum reproaching her. He had been listening to her plan and was astounded that she wanted to offer help to the brutal white men. Pocahontas was disappointed. It was exactly this attitude that had made her determined to keep her plan secret. Her people had simply jumped to the wrong conclusion about the visitors.

Ignoring Kocoum's warnings about the settlers, Pocahontas went to meet John Smith. The soldier was overjoyed to see Pocahontas, but worried that their secret meeting was dangerous for her. She told him that the settlement's problems were a cause for more concern. John Smith insisted that they would survive the winter on what they had, then turned away. Pocahontas was right: they barely had enough food to last them until Christmas, never mind the cold months to follow. There was no point admitting it to Pocahontas, though. After all, what would she be able to do about it? The two shouldn't even have been talking to each other!

Pocahontas sensed that John Smith was simply being brave, as he had been trained to be, and decided to prove to him that she had an easy solution to his problem. Having told him to follow her, Pocahontas led the puzzled Captain to the storehouse and stepped aside to let him see the plentiful supplies within.

John Smith gaped at the huge piles of food that filled the storehouse as Pocahontas told him of their successful harvest. There were mounds of grain, hillocks of vegetables and basketfuls of things he'd never even seen before in his life! The Indians truly did know how to live in harmony with the land; they would surely not get through all this food before the spring?

As Meeko and Percy eagerly scampered over to a mountain of food to sample it,

Pocahontas suggested that John Smith take some of the surplus to the visitors' stores. No one would know, so no one would object! John Smith thought it an excellent idea and thanked Pocahontas for her kindness. As always, Pocahontas needed no thanks and paid attention instead to hungry little Meeko, who was scrabbling around in one of the vegetable baskets. John Smith decided that the provisions should be transferred at night and said he would bring a cart from the settlement the next evening.

Their arrangements made, Pocahontas and John Smith agreed to meet again at sunset the following day. Having said goodbye, the soldier strode jauntily away, happy in the knowledge that his men would soon have plenty to eat. Christmas might not be so bad after all! At his side struggled Percy, his mouth stuffed with a cob of corn that he had taken from the storehouse. Pocahontas watched them both leave until they had disappeared into the distance, then headed for home.

Kocoum had seen everything and shook his head incredulously at the sight of the Chief's daughter talking with a settler. The white man was bound to be deceiving her: all settlers were dangerous as far as the Indian was concerned. He had to do something to protect Pocahontas. He would follow her to her next meeting with the soldier, so he could be there to save her from coming to any harm. Having made up his mind, Kocoum, too, darted through the trees back towards his village.

Late that night, Ratcliffe made a moonlit trip to his private food supply. The sound of his heavy footsteps on the wooden deck echoed emptily round the still bay. He greedily rubbed his hands together and licked his lips as he looked at all the delicious treats before him, wondering what he should eat first. He chuckled with delight as he relished the fact that all the food belonged to him. Only Percy would be allowed to share it. There was more than enough to last them the whole winter.

He swept his dog up in his fat arms so that he could feed him a little treat, only to find that Percy's mouth was already full. But what was it full of? Keeping his jaws clamped around the cob, Percy let out a guilty little whimper. His master snatched up the unfamiliar object and examined it under the bright light of the moon. His eyes narrowed. It was food, there was no doubt about that, but it wasn't English food. He sniffed at it. It smelled rather pleasant. Where could his dog have picked up such a strange vegetable?

Ratcliffe demanded where Percy had found the vegetable. Percy merely trembled at his master's raised voice and whined pitifully. The Governor held the cob up to his face again and frowned. The only explanation was that the food had somehow come from the Indians. It was impossible to get near their village, never mind their food stores, so someone must have been allowed in there. Ratcliffe rubbed his flabby chin thoughtfully. John Smith was always jabbering on about friendly deals with those savages. He was sure to have something to do with this!

The next evening, John Smith came to collect the food from the Indian village. He piled up as many supplies as he could manage and thanked Pocahontas again. She had come to their rescue just in time! The settlers were having enough problems getting to used to living in a strange country; the last thing they needed to worry about was where their next meal was coming from, especially near Christmastime.

John Smith was about to take his laden wagon back to the settlement, when he was startled by the sound of Ratcliffe's booming voice behind him. He spun round to find himself looking down the barrel of the Governor's shotgun and for a moment could not speak. Furious though he was, Ratcliffe kept the gun steady as he pointed it straight at John Smith. He had already told this soldier to keep away from the savages. Backing away slightly, John Smith explained that the Indians were only being friendly and were offering badly needed supplies of food. Ratcliffe angrily jabbed the barrel of his gun in John Smith's chest and rebuked him for being so gullible. The Indians were their enemies, why would they offer any kind of help? This whole food business was nothing but an elaborate trap, and the Captain had fallen right into it. The Indians couldn't match the settlers' firearms with their primitive weapons, so they were using poisoned food instead! They were trying to protect the gold stores, to keep all the treasure for themselves!

This terrible accusation was too much for Kocoum to tolerate. He had followed Pocahontas as planned and had been watching the dispute between the two settlers with interest. When he heard his people being spoken of in such a disrespectful way, he sprang from his hiding place to defend their honour. Raising his tomahawk menacingly above his head, Kocoum bellowed at Ratcliffe and sped towards him. Pocahontas and John Smith gasped and watched helplessly as the Indian warrior ran right into the path of Ratcliffe's shotgun. He couldn't possibly get to his enemy before the gun went off!

Just as the Governor took aim, his dog rushed towards Kocoum and sank his sharp little teeth into the Indian's leg to protect his master. Kocoum had suffered many battle injuries in his life, but the strange animal took him by surprise. As he cried out and looked to see what had bitten him, his weapon flew from his hand and spun towards Ratcliffe.

Ratcliffe heard a dull thud as the tomahawk embedded itself in the side of the wagon, inches from his face. He shrieked and was momentarily unable to move as he saw how sharp the metal blade was. If that had hit him... He dismissed the thought, remembering that the Indian was now unarmed and disabled: an easy target. With a chilling sneer, the Governor prepared to take aim again. Suddenly, he was distracted by something fluttering around his face. It was flying so fast, he couldn't even see what it

was. He lashed out at the creature to frighten it off, but it dodged him easily and even hovered for a brief moment as if to mock him. He could see then that it was a brightly coloured bird. Spurred on by Pocahontas, it was quickly off again, speeding round and round his head like a troublesome fly. Ratcliffe made another effort to shoo Flit away. As he tottered and waved his gun around vigorously, a shot fired, sending a bullet clean through the wagon rope. There was a moment's silence, then a creak of wooden wheels.

The loaded wagon had been secured on a hill and began to hurtle towards Ratcliffe. The startled Governor dropped his gun and began to run clumsily down the hill. He raced down towards the settlement, yelling for help, with the cart relentlessly following. John Smith stood amazed for a second, then sped after them. He was joined by Pocahontas, who ignored Kocoum's pleas to stay behind.

The commotion brought the settlers to the entrance, just in time for them to see their wild-eyed governor dart through the gate, moments before a heavy wagon crashed into it. The cart toppled over, spilling its huge load across the ground. The men gasped and stared at the food mountain. They fell to their knees before it to get a closer look. Just as they were having to ration their food, a mound of supplies had descended upon them! It was truly a miracle! Now they could all look forward to a real Christmas celebration, just like the ones they had at home.

Embarrassed by the whole affair, Ratcliffe kept out of sight for the rest of the day, claiming that he had a headache. Once he was sure that his men were sleeping soundly, he abruptly awoke his servant, Wiggins, and demanded that he take him to the ship. Wiggins groaned, but sleepily obliged. He was interested to know the reason for their midnight rowing trip. By now, Ratcliffe was ravenous, and told Wiggins of his secret food store. He could hardly wait to board the ship and get stuck in!

Wiggins followed his master down the deck. If he bowed and scraped enough, the master might even share some food with him! Ratcliffe opened the door expectantly, then began to shake with anger. All his food had disappeared! Amongst the few crumbs that remained sat Meeko and Percy. They had eaten the whole lot between them! Percy gulped and stared pitifully up at his master, pleading forgiveness. Meeko glanced at the Governor, then calmly finished his biscuit before being chased away.

Ratcliffe ranted at Meeko and Percy as he chased them round the ship. The animals finally made their escape by jumping overboard, landing in the rowing boat. Thinking they were safe, they looked back at the ship, only to find that the Governor had picked up a barrel ready to hurl at them. They had no choice but to jump into the cold sea. Wiggins could see what was about to happen and tried to stop his master, but Ratcliffe was deaf as well as blind with rage. With a roar, he hurled the barrel on to the rowing boat,

splitting it in two. Crestfallen, Wiggins put his hands to his head, then peeped over the side. Their only means of getting back to land was now only good for firewood. They were stranded until morning.

Meanwhile, the settlement's Christmas celebrations had begun as the men made a start on some of the delicious treats given by the Indians. Pocahontas saw the happiness on the men's faces and turned to smile at John Smith.

As the men ate and drank to their heart's content, the Governor and Wiggins sat on the ship in silence. The sound of merry singing reached them across the water as Wiggins bit into a tasteless ship's biscuit and offered one to his master. Ratcliffe snatched it from his hand and threw it across the floor in a sulk. This was a fine way for a Governor to spend Christmas!

John Smith assured Pocahontas that this was a special time of year for the men, and that was why he had allowed them such a luxurious spread to celebrate it. He did not want her to think that this was how much the men normally ate, otherwise she would insist on bringing another cartload of food! Pocahontas was curious and wanted to know more about the celebration the settlers called Christmas, but John Smith assured her that there was no need. After all, Christmas was a time for giving, and Pocahontas had shown that she knew all there was to know about that....

A page for
you to
colour